Quincy
Moves to the Desert

Camille Matthews
with illustrations by **Michelle Black**

Text, Illustrations and Entire Publication
Copyright © 2011 by Pathfinder Equine Publications, LLC

Illustrations by Michelle Black

Published by Pathfinder Equine Publications
243 N. Garfield Rd.
Mohrsville, PA 19541
Camille Matthews: pathfinder1908@gmail.com

ISBN: 978-0-9819240-1-4

CPSIA Compliance Information: Batch 0311
For further information contact
RJ Communications
Phone 800 621-2556

Printed in the USA

The QUINCY THE HORSE books
are for my grandfather,
William L. Matthews, Sr.
my mentor,
Phyllis E. Schiff
and
my daughter, Lisa

—Camille Matthews

Quincy was a little red horse.

His coat was the color of a new penny.

His mane and tail were long and shiny.

His eyes were soft and brown.

On his nose was a long white blaze.

Quincy lived in a tan and white barn.

There were many horses in the tan and white barn. Quincy's best friend was an old brown horse named Beau. Beau liked to talk and tell Quincy about the places he had been and the things he had done. When Quincy had a problem, he could talk to Beau.

A man named George owned the tan and white barn. He was good to the horses who lived there. He taught horses and people to ride. Quincy liked to see George and Beau stand at the fence and watch him trot around the ring behind the tan and white barn.

George's barn had lots of things that horses need. There were brushes for grooming and picks for cleaning feet. There were racks for saddles and hooks for bridles. There was a shelf for medicine if a horse got sick. Quincy was happy in the tan and white barn.

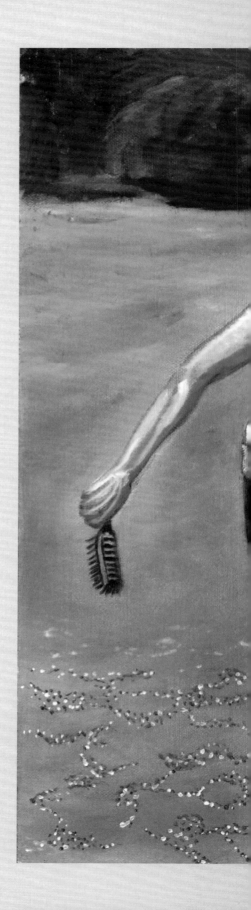

Quincy's owner was a lady named Cam. She was Beau's owner too. She lived in town, but she came to ride them almost every day.

She combed their manes and brushed their tails. She cleaned their bridles and polished their saddles. Sometimes she even brought them apples.

Quincy loved Cam!

One afternoon Cam came to the barn.

It was almost dark. It was too late to ride.

She did not stop at Quincy's stall. She went over to Beau.

She opened the door of his stall and went inside.

Quincy wondered what she was saying to Beau.

Suddenly Quincy heard another sound.

The feed cart was coming.

It was time for HAY and OATS.

Quincy loved HAY and OATS!

He would wait to find out what Cam was saying to Beau.

When he had eaten, Quincy turned and peered through the bars at Beau. Beau came to the wall near Quincy and said, "We are going on a big trip. We are going to the desert far away from here."

A Big Trip? The Desert?

Quincy had never been on a big trip. He had never gone far away or seen a desert. He asked Beau, "Are there horses in the desert?"

Beau laughed. "Horses are everywhere," he said.

Then Quincy asked, "Why do we need to go far away?"

Beau said, "The desert is in the West. The West has wide open spaces and trails as far as you can see." Quincy could not picture the trails in the desert. The only trails he had ever seen were in the forest near the farm where he used to live.

The Beau said, "There are many things to see in this big country. We will have a great trip! Now let's go to sleep."

Soon the day came for the big trip.

George led Quincy and Beau through the barn door.

In the driveway was the biggest truck Quincy had ever seen.

It had windows and a big ramp that hit the ground with a BANG!

George walked Quincy and Beau up the ramp and tied them in stalls. It was time to say goodbye. George patted Quincy and hugged Beau. He said, "Don't worry. The driver will take good care of you." Then he pushed in the ramp and pulled the big door shut.

The big truck drove down the highway.

Sometimes the road was smooth.

SWISH...SWISH...SWISH

Sometimes the road was bumpy.

CLUNK! CLUNK! CLUNK!

Sometimes Quincy took a nap.

Sometimes Quincy stretched his neck.

He looked out the window to see what he

could see.

As they rode across the country, Beau told Quincy about the places they saw. He told Quincy that the country has many states and that each state has a name. Every day they were going to drive through new states.

On the first day the truck left New York and came to Pennsylvania.

Out of the window Quincy saw a strange sight. A man in a yellow straw hat was using a team of horses to farm a field.

Beau said, "Those are draft horses. They are big and strong. They like to pull."

Beau told Quincy that the man in the hat was an Amish farmer. Beau said the Amish work hard, but they do not use tractors or cars. They need horses to do their work and even to drive their buggies down the road!

Quincy wondered if he could pull like that.

Each night the truck stopped and the horses got off. They had stalls in a barn where they could lie down and sleep. Soon Beau told Quincy they had left Pennsylvania and passed through Ohio. The truck was coming to Kentucky.

Beau said, "Kentucky is the home of the racehorse. Many racehorses are Thoroughbreds. They are fast. They like to run." Beau told Quincy about the starting gate and cheering crowds. He told Quincy about the winner's circle and the big silver trophy.

That night Quincy dreamed he was a racehorse coming down the track.

The next morning, Beau told Quincy about many other kinds of horses. He told Quincy about Standardbreds with their heads held high. He told Quincy about Arabian horses in beautiful costumes, Gypsy Vanners with long hair on their feet, Appaloosas with spots, and golden Palominos and Paints.

Next the truck turned West. It went through Missouri, Kansas and Oklahoma. This was the longest day on the road.

Quincy was getting tired of this big trip. He was tired of learning about new states and different kinds of horses. He missed New York. He missed George and the tan and white barn. Most of all he missed Cam.

Quincy asked Beau, "Where is Cam?" Beau said, "Don't worry. We will see her soon."

Quincy felt excited. He hoped Beau was right.

At the end of the day the truck came to the state of Texas. It stopped at a red and white barn called the Happy Trails Horse Motel. The driver led Quincy and Beau down the ramp and tied them to the trailer.

Beau was so excited that he could hardly stand still. He told Quincy that Texas was the state where he was born.

Quincy was surprised. He said, "I thought New York was your home."

Beau said, "Texas is the home of the American Quarterhorse. I am an American Quarterhorse. I took a big trip to New York a long time ago."

Then Beau said, "Texas is also the home of the Western horse. Many Western horses are American Quarterhorses. They are smart and they like to work. An American Quarterhorse can do anything."

Beau told Quincy about cowboys and cowgirls. He told Quincy about rodeos with calf roping, bucking broncos, barrel racing and bull riding. He told Quincy about long rides on winding trails that went as far as a horse could see.

Quincy decided he was going to rope a calf!

That night before they fell asleep, Quincy thought about the places he had seen and the states he had crossed.

Quincy asked Beau, "What state is the desert in?" Beau answered, "The desert is in New Mexico."

Then Quincy thought about all the different kinds of horses he'd seen and their different jobs. He knew that every horse needs a job. Quincy asked Beau the most important question of all. "What kind of horse am I? What kind of job will there be for me in New Mexico?"

Beau said, "You are an American Quarterhorse, just like me. A good Quarterhorse can do anything."

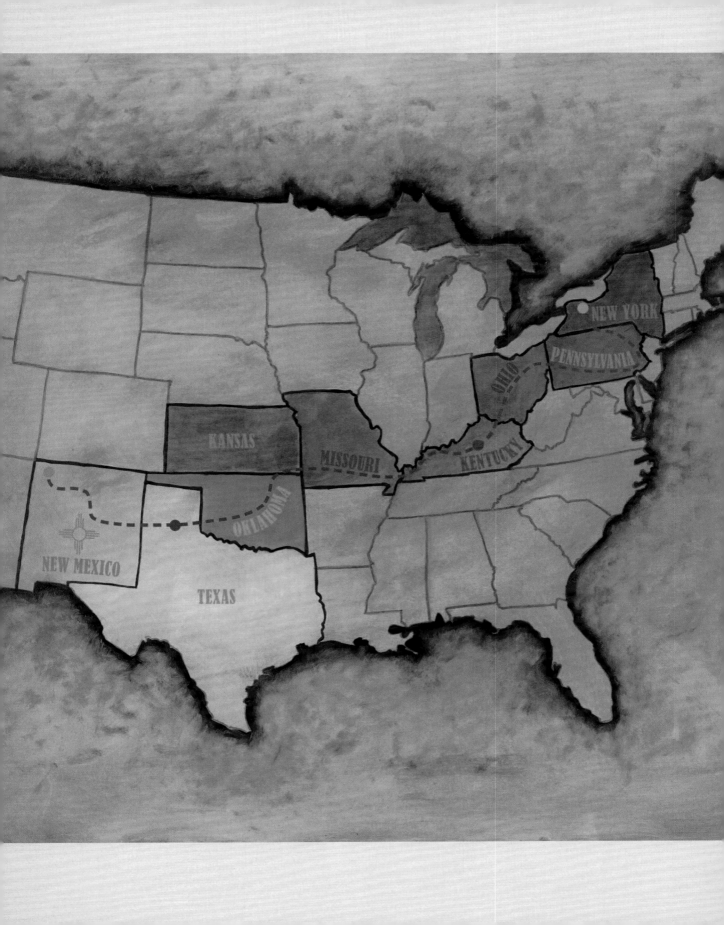

The next morning the driver led them up the ramp. The truck turned onto the highway for the very last day. When Quincy looked out, he saw a beautiful sight.

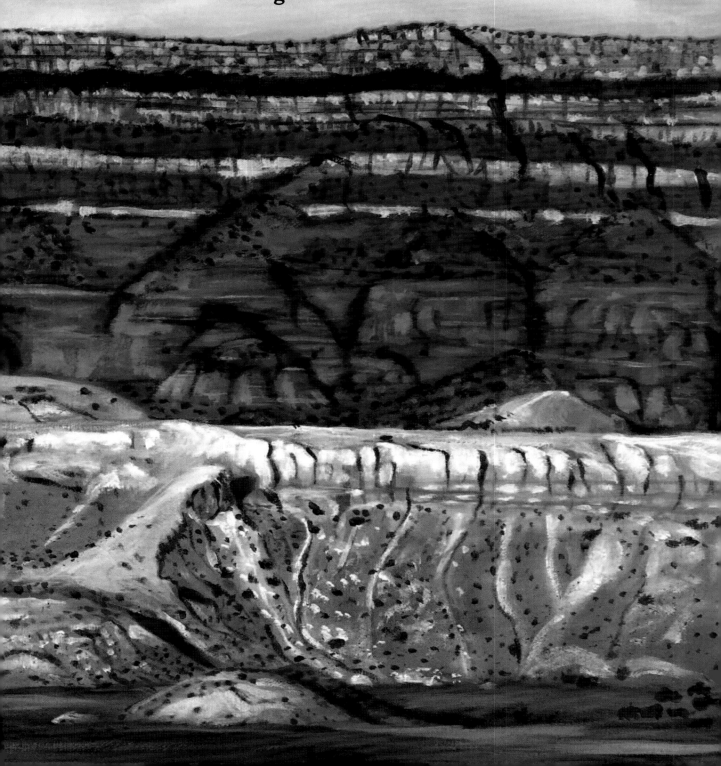

Quincy saw sky that was blue and cliffs that were red. He saw rocks that were white and trees that were green. There was a trail stretching across the desert as far as he could see.

Finally the truck slowed down and rolled to a stop. The driver opened the big door and pulled out the ramp. Quincy looked at Beau and then he looked out. At the bottom of the ramp stood Cam. She led Quincy out of the trailer onto the desert sand.

He was so happy he did not know what to do.